Stay Sweet !

Chyful Clart
1/16/23

A LESSON A DAY

A Child's Way

BY CHERYL WILLIAMS

DORRANCE
PUBLISHING CO
EST. 1920
PITTSBURGH, PENNSYLVANIA 15238

Dorrance Publishing Co
585 Alpha Drive
Suite 103
Pittsburgh, PA 15238
Visit our website at *www.dorrancebookstore.com*

ISBN: 978-1-6386-7158-9
eISBN: 978-1-6386-7691-1

A LESSON A DAY

A Child's Way

Table of Contents

1. Is It True?. 7

2. You Can Do It 9

3. Change 10

4. What Do You See? 11

5. Baby Bear's Day on the Town. 13

6. Mr. Skunk said Mr. Rabbit 14

7. Baby Duck's Decision 17

8. Healthy for Me 18

9. True Friendship 19

10. Beaver's Dam 21

11. Snowy Memories 23

12. Waiting your turn 24

13. Where is Mr. Ferret 27

14. Honey Party 28

15. The Four-Legged Chair 29

16. The Geese Unite. 31

17. An Unexpected Friend. 32

18. Hygiene. 33

19. The Honey Bees 35

20. Beautiful Bubbly Bub 36

21. The Mask 37

22. The Orca's Adventure 39

23. Sharing is Love. 40

24. The Beaver's Way. 41

Dedicated to all the beautiful children around the world

1. Is It True?

"Oh my! Oh my!" yelled mother hen.
"Who on earth stole my eggs?
I know it must be Lizard
As he was here today
He did, I know he did it
Even though I didn't see him."

"Why do you think he stole your eggs?"
The Blue Jay butted in
"You said you didn't see him, hen,
So why do you think he did?
You shouldn't just say things that you think
Or you can hurt his feelings
Don't just assume he took them, hen.
Ask lizard if he did."

2. You Can Do It

"I can't do it, Mr. Fox
I'm just not smart enough
I am not as big and strong as you
So I might as well just give up."

"Oh, yes you can, my squirrel friend
You can do it certainly
You may not be as strong and tough as me
But you are very smart, you see

"You build your home up in the tree
And keep your babies safe
You save up food for winter days
And help trees populate

"Don't say that you're not smart enough
You don't have to be like me
And just between the two of us

You are pretty smart to me."

3. Change

The caterpillar spins and spins
Working tirelessly all day

Never ever settling
On staying the same way

He knows that it's not easy
And easy is not his way

He must work each day
To make a change
So one day he'll fly away

He knows that change brings beauty
Though at times it's hard to see

Without change there will be no butterflies
And he'll never ever learn to fly

4. What Do You See?

"It's a beautiful day
It's a beautiful day,
Croaks Tammy Green Frog
As she hops away
Oh, what a beautiful day it is today."

"It looks cold and gray and dreary,
The old grumpy bat declared
All I see are dark clouds everywhere,
And I'm sure it's going to rain."

"I know that it might rain today,
Croaks Tammy Frog, hopping away
But beauty is what you imagine it
Even if it rains and rains all day."

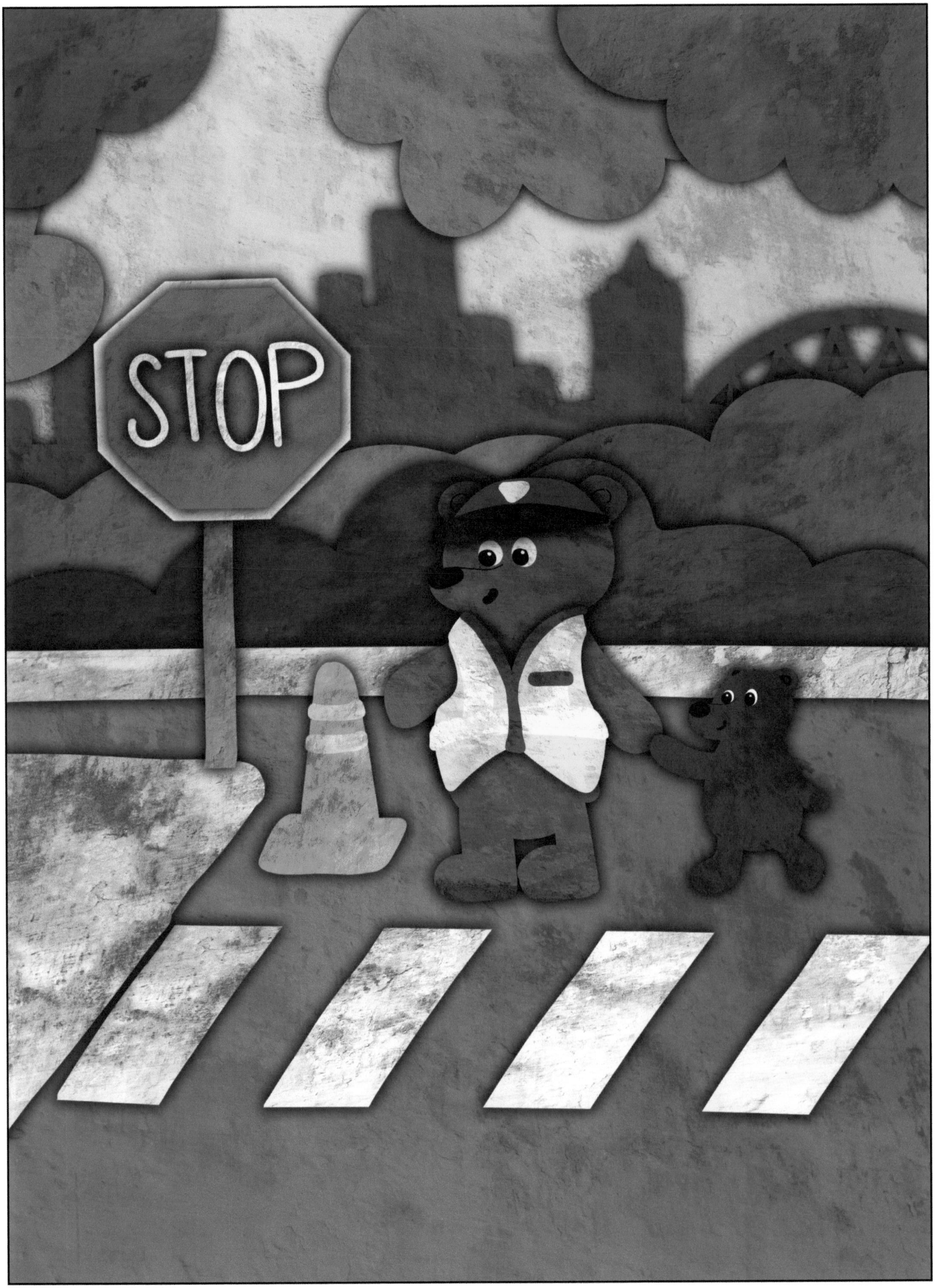
STOP

5. Baby Bear's Day on the Town

Baby bear stopped and looked around
That big old scary town

And suddenly started to frown

Mama bear had told him time and time again
To stay at home, and never venture out alone

But time and time again her warnings he ignored

Now he was caught in a scary situation
Running around all alone in an unfamiliar town

Luckily a crossing guard noticed a little bear
With his head hanging down
Looking sadly at the ground

Finally little bear was found

That day he learned a very important lesson
To always listen to his mom

6. Mr. Skunk said Mr. Rabbit

Mr. Rabbit was so furry white
With fiery red eyes

On his back, Mr. Skunk had white stripes
And was blacker than the night

"Mr. Skunk," said Mr. Rabbit
Why on earth are you so black?
I can hardly ever see you when you're outside in the dark."

"Yes, I'm black, Mr. Rabbit," responded Mr. Skunk
But my color makes me so unique
Cause I'm made unique like that

"Mr. Skunk," said Mr. Rabbit
What are those stripes up on your back?"

"I will tell you, Mr. Rabbit,
Mr. Skunk then answered back
It might seem weird to look at
But those stripes make me look so unique
And I'm made unique like that."

"Mr. Skunk," said Mr. Rabbit
Why don't you look like me?"

"Well, my friend, you are a rabbit, and I am a skunk, you see
Even though we do look different, and are made so differently
We are both unique in every way
As unique as we can be."

7. Baby Duck's Decision

Baby duck was too afraid
Too afraid to learn to swim
So whenever they head to the lake
On dry land he would stay

The other little ducklings
Kept making fun of him
Even though they hurt his feelings
He still would not give in

One cool Sunday afternoon
On his favorite spot he sat
Watching all the other ducklings
Busy doing swimming laps
They were having loads and loads of fun
As they laughed and played all day

Baby duck watched on
Feeling so annoyed
Thinking that this would be the last…
The last day he sat upon that grass

8. Healthy for Me

"Why are you shunning me?"
Asked the broccoli ever so loudly

"You love the beef
The fries and sweets
But you never seem to like me."

"Why do you never drink me?"
Asked the water repeatedly
"You drink the juice
And soda too
But you never seem to like me.

"Drinking water is so good for you
Eating broccoli
Keeps you healthy too

"There's no need for you to make a fuss
You can still eat all the things you love
Don't overfill those bellies, though
Please save some room for us."

9. True Friendship

That Sendy Dog and Pennie Cat
A special love was all they had
They didn't care what others had to say
Their friendship was special in every way

When Sendy Dog had lost her pups
Pennie Cat did have her back

When Pennie Cat
Had hurt her paw
Sendy Dog had helped her cause

Though Pennie and Sendy didn't look the same
The same blood was running through their veins

They loved each other in every way
Despite what others had to say

10. Beaver's Dam

The Beaver worked and worked all day
Building his dam his own way
Then along came Mr. Red fish
Who wasn't liking it

He didn't like the endless sticks
And the dirty muddy paste
He didn't care for anything
But to put his two cents in

"What do you think you are doing?"
He finally declared
You are ruining the whole thing
Stop adding all those twigs."

"Mr. Fish, you should stay out of it,"
The wise Owl butted in
"It's the way the Beaver likes it
And it's really up to him."

11. Snowy Memories

The snowman stands and looks around
Fixing his snowy gear
Laughing playfully at all the kids
Throwing snowballs in the air

He doesn't just sit and wait around
For anyone's permission
But blends in with the snowy hill
The air which snowflakes filled

He raises his brows
And straightens his orange nose
Flashing a smile big and round
Admiring the kids frolicking
On the snowy ground

He knows his days are numbered
He knows his nights are too
So he wants to spend every second
Making memories with you

12. Waiting your turn

Mr. Alligator wanted to be first
To be first at any cost

He would push his way up to the front
Not caring whose toes he stepped on

The animals were so afraid of him
That they'd always let him have his way

Then one day a Mr. Crocodile came to town
To visit and to play

It was a festive time of year
And all the animals came from far and near

Waiting at the amusement park, standing on line
Purchasing their tickets to get onto the rides

First in line was Mr. Crocodile
Followed by Miss Lilly Frog

Then along came Mr. Alligator
Yelling at the top of his lungs

"I'm always, always first, I say
So get out of my way!"

The other animals were afraid of him
So they just let him win

But Mr. Crocodile didn't even budge
Or let him have his way

First in line is where he was
And first in line he stayed

13. Where is Mr. Ferret

Mr. Ferret woke up to the sounds
Of loud voices all around

All he saw were eyes and noses
Where on earth could he be now?

The last thing that he remembered
Was the pet store down the street

Now he woke up in a strange place
With no clue where he might be

Can you help out Mr. Ferret
As he figures out this place?

Can you tell him where his home is?
A place filled with desks and chairs

14. Honey Party

We moved to the country
Honeycomb county
My mother, my sister
My brother and me

So many weren't very neighborly
And making friends sure wasn't easy

We buzzed around from tree to tree
Only finding one that could be
A very sweet, sweet Buzzy Bee

Then Buzzy Bee invited me
To Bunny Bee's honey party
A honey party for three
Buzzing together, two honey bees and me

Finally, neighbors who were neighborly
Making good buzzing memories
At Bunny Bee's honey party

15. The Four-Legged Chair

Chairs are made for sitting
They bear the load we wear
Yet never start complaining
That the weight's too much to bear

That chair we take for granted
May be useless some may say
But can you just imagine
If we had to stand all day?

When our legs become so weary
And the pressure we can't bear
We can know release is certain
When we sit upon that chair

So don't ever take for granted
The importance of a chair
As it always keeps on giving
Even when we fail to care

16. The Geese Unite

All the different sounds
As they slowly paced around
In all the different sizes
Heading toward the playground

All the unique feathers
In all the different numbers
In a V-shaped flight
Flying high across the sky

All the different geese
With all the same webbed feet
Lining up with glee
Ready for a playground spree

They all go marching one behind the other
Marching on together
Basking in the warmth of the sun
Together enjoying a day of fun

17. An Unexpected Friend

My name is Dannie Frog
I used to live in a nearby swamp
With my cousin Dranzie
And my baby sister Oozie
Now we recently moved to a new city
For a few months with my uncle Froglee

The first day of my new school
Wasn't very cool
It appeared that the other frogs
Didn't want me around

I sat there in class all by myself
With not even a bullfrog
Introducing himself
Looking around at all the rest
At the other frogs sitting quietly at their desks

Just when the silence seemed to last
A bullfrog way in the back
Whispered, "Hello, and welcome to class."

18. Hygiene

The soap and tap are ready for messy hands and feet
For smelly arms and sweaty cheeks
Getting bodies squeaky clean

The brush and paste are both in place
To clean those teeth after you've ate

This important task we call hygiene
Preventing cavities

Now you're awake, it's time again
To wash those hands and cheeks

To brush those teeth
So they are nice and clean
Now breakfast you will eat

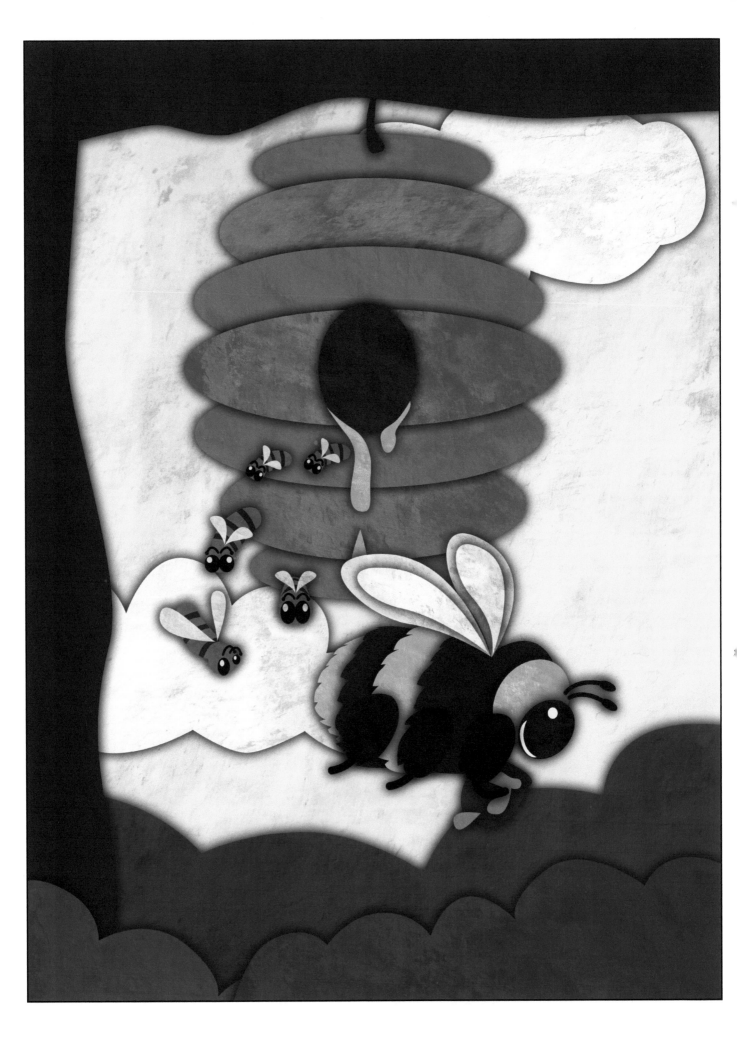

19. The Honey Bees

The honey bees just loved to be
On the honeycomb dripped in honey

Then along came Mr. Bumble Bee
Eyes filled with greed
With plans to steal honey as far
As the eyes could see

The bumble bee was greedy
As greedy as can be
He didn't want to work so hard
He wanted it all for free

But the honey bees buzzed loudly
As loudly as can be
They worked together as a team
To defeat that bumble bee

20. Beautiful Bubbly Bub

Flying up so very high
Different shapes and colors
Rising up into the sky

Floating one behind the other
Spreading love all over

Some of them in even
And others in odd numbers

Bringing fun to everyone
Laughter echoing with joyful sounds
As the bubbles keep bursting one by one

Empty bottles spread out on the ground
As they quickly make their way out

Brightening up the whole atmosphere
Rising so high up in the air

21. The Mask

The blue mask hangs on the shower wall
After a long hard day at work
Covering mouths and noses
In different sizes big and small

So many think he is useless
And he isn't worth a thing
Others think that he's a savior
From whatever germs may bring

As he hangs there on the shower wall
With his brothers green, black, gray, and mauve
Hoping more will one day see his role
And appreciate his worth

The green mask hangs on the shower wall
All clean and ready for work
To hug those mouths and noses close
And keep away those germs

22. The Orca's Adventure

The Orca whale just set sail
On an ocean adventure far away

An adventure to go anywhere
Anywhere in the ocean
Just to make it clear

He packed his bags
With enough to last
In case he faced hard times

He didn't want to head back home
Before the time was right
The Orca whale said his goodbyes
And promised he would write

Even though he'll miss his family so
He was excited to explore
Ready to take on a whole new world
And the challenges in store

23. Sharing is Love

The yellow cows ate quietly
In the open fields with glee

There was so much grass for all to eat
But the orange cows were greedy

They came along and chased them off
Taking more than was their share

The dogs looked on at what went on
And saw it wasn't fair

So they stood up for the yellow cows
And chased the orange cows away

24. The Beaver's Way

Baby beaver was an imitator
Who always wanted to be
As strong as his big brother

But he didn't like trying very much
As the other animals always laughed at him
Whenever he messed up

At times he got so angry
And felt he couldn't succeed

But Mama beaver always helped him see
That he should never let anyone make him feel

That he couldn't become the strongest beaver
That he could possibly be

CPSIA information can be obtained
at www.ICGtesting.com
Printed in the USA
BVHW022054021122
650438BV00004B/18